To Eimer, who I have shared many good and bad hair days with, and Andy, who once told me my hair would make the perfect nest

Library of Congress Cataloging-in-Publication data is on file with the publisher.

First published in 2017 by Macmillan Children's Books,
an imprint of Pan Macmillan, a division of Macmillan Publishers International Limited.
Text and illustrations copyright © Gemma Merino
Published in 2017 by Albert Whitman & Company
ISBN 978-0-8075-7338-9
Printed in China
10 9 8 7 6 5 4 3 2 1 WKT 20 19 18 17 16

For more information about Albert Whitman & Company,
visit our web site at www.albertwhitman.com.

THE SHEEP WHO HATCHED AN EGG

Gemma Merino

ALBERT WHITMAN & COMPANY
CHICAGO, ILLINOIS

Lola the sheep had extraordinary wool.
It was shiny, it was silky, it was soft,
and it never, ever tangled.

Lola spent hours washing, drying, and brushing
her wool to make it absolutely perfect.

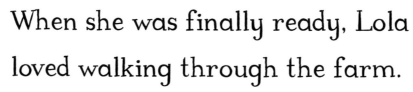

When she was finally ready, Lola
loved walking through the farm.

"Isn't she beautiful?"

"Isn't she perfect?"

"Isn't her wool extraordinary?"

said all the other sheep.

And Lola felt proud and happy.

But one hot day,
something terrible happened.

All the sheep had
to have a haircut...

...and Lola's extraordinary wool was gone!

"Now you'll feel
nice and cool,"
said the dog.

But Lola felt ridiculous without her shiny, silky wool.

All she wanted to do was hide.

So off she went to
the far side of the hill,
where she waited

and waited

and waited.

Little by little,
her wool grew back.

But...

...Lola's wool didn't grow back shiny or silky. It wasn't even soft!

It was wild, it was messy,

and it **tangled!**

"It's HORRIBLE!"

cried Lola.

Just then, a small,
delicate egg landed
on Lola's head.

But her wool was now so thick
that she didn't even notice!

That night was very cold, but the little egg was safe and snug, wrapped in Lola's messy wool.

And there it stayed, until...

...Lola woke to find a small,
excited chick sitting on her head!

Lola loved the chick's colorful feathers and its beautiful songs.

And the chick loved Lola's kindness and her very messy wool.

"It's so fluffy."

"It's so warm."

"Your wool is extraordinary!"

said the chick each night.

And Lola felt proud and happy
to have helped her little friend.

Lola and the chick had
so much fun together.

Each day the chick grew
bigger and stronger.

And Lola grew bigger and fluffier!

But the days were getting hotter and hotter...

"I need a haircut," puffed Lola.

"And I need to see the world," sang the bird.

They both knew it was time to say good-bye.

The next day, they wished each other
good luck and hoped they'd meet again.

Lola returned to the farm.
She didn't look perfect,
but it didn't matter.

She was so happy to
see her friends!

Now Lola felt nice and cool, and she no longer missed her shiny, silky wool.

This time, when it grew back,
she hoped it would be wilder and
fluffier than ever before...

...and it was.